THE JOURNAL OF MILO THATCH

PROPERTY OF
Whitmore
Industries
Preston B. Whitmore Archives

Personal and Confidential

THE JOURNAL OF MILO THATCH

Assembled, preserved, and
annotated by Preston B. Whitmore

a Welcome book

DISNEY

EDITIONS

New York

Personal and Confidential

0-7868-5341-7

Library of Congress Cataloging-in-Publication
Data available upon request.

For information address
Disney Editions
114 Fifth Avenue
New York, New York 10011-5690

Produced by:
Welcome Enterprises, Inc.
588 Broadway, Suite 303
New York, New York 10012

Project Manager: Jacinta O'Halloran
Designer: Jon Glick
Design Assistant: Naomi Irie
Disney Editions Editorial Director: Wendy Lefkon
Disney Editions Senior Editor: Sara Baysinger
Disney Editions Assistant Editor: Jody Revenson

Printed in China

First Edition

10 9 8 7 6 5 4 3 2 1

Visit www.disneyeditions.com

 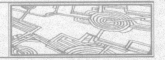
INTRODUCTION
MEET MILO THATCH

An explanation of this unusual volume,
and an appreciation of its author,
by Preston B. Whitmore

To Posterity:

In order to fully grasp the contents of this volume,
one must first attempt to understand its author--
Milo James Thatch. And, in order to understand Milo,
one must be familiar with the man who was his
greatest influence--his grandfather, Thaddeus T.
Thatch.

   It was my great fortune in my youth--many years
ago at Georgetown--to make Thaddeus' acquaintance.
And while Thatch and I were fueled by very disparate
passions, our mutual respect led us to forge a
lasting bond. I would bore him with stories of
railroad fortunes, factories, and industrial
development, and he would retort with theories of
lost civilizations: the Anasazi, Lemuria, Mu, and,
of course, his obsession, Atlantis. To the end of
his days (against much opposition), Thatch
maintained that the key to finding the lost empire
of Atlantis lay in the pages of a book called the
Shepherd's Journal. I even made a much-publicized
bet with Thatch that if he ever found the so-called

Shepherd's Journal that I would not only fund
his expedition to Atlantis, but I would kiss
him full on the mouth. Imagine my embarrassment
when he found the darn thing.

The story of Atlantis is history's greatest
jigsaw puzzle, but Thatch's passion and his
superior intellect held him in good stead and
we are now the beneficiaries of his years of
research and sleuthing. Thatch's documents,
along with the work of his fine grandson, Milo,
have withstood time and scholastic scrutiny
(including an exhaustive factual audit by the
New England Academic Consortium) to become
recognized as the definitive history of the
lost empire.

Although Milo Thatch grew up in the shadow
of his renowned grandfather, the younger Thatch
achieved greatness in his own right, even
surpassing the legendary accomplishments of his
grandfather, with the discovery of the lost
empire of Atlantis. Milo was educated as a
cartographer and linguist, and held nominal
employment with the world's leading historical
institution in such capacity from 1903 to 1914.
Although Milo was an expert in cartography, his
greatest skill lay in translation. He held a
double doctorate in both linguistic theory and

dead languages and was known to be fluent or
near-fluent in Choctaw, Pima, Hopi, Tlingit,
several Bantu tongues, Siamese, Cantonese,
Welsh, Old Norse, Egyptian, Sumerian,
Thessolonian, and Atlantean.

This remarkable document came into my
possession some time ago. To Milo's credit and
the world's advantage, his journal reveals its
author's great capacity to retain facts and
recall conversations with assuredness. As can
only be expected of a great historian, Milo
recorded his amazing experiences to the last
detail. While I have hesitated to reveal the
explosive secrets this journal contains by
publishing it in toto, I felt it my duty to
edit the journal itself, and to organize and
annotate its contents to the best of my
ability, in the hope that those who might be
privy to its contents in future centuries might
have a thorough understanding not only of the
wonders of Atlantis, but of the remarkable
young man who was so much a part of its
discovery.

Regards,

Preston B. Whitmore

Preston B. Whitmore and Thaddeus T. Thatch

Whitmore Industries

PART ONE
REJECTION AND RECOGNITION
An academic rebuke is followed
by an unexpected and intriguing proposal.

The fascinating journal of Milo J. Thatch
begins in the fall of 1914. As a preface to
the events he will outline in the subsequent
pages, it should be understood that Thatch at
this time endured a mounting frustration after
his decade of historical researches. In an
effort to quash his uncommon skills, desire,
and enthusiasm, his so-called superiors had
perpetually assigned him the most menial of
tasks. Thatch persevered, because he naively
believed that the credibility of his
scientific knowledge would ultimately win over
his skeptical supervisors.

He was yet unacquainted with the inequities
of the world, where mighty bureaucracies exist
under the control of timorous little men. To
these men, the thought of innovative thinking
is not looked upon with fervor, but as a
threat to hard-won power--power that they are
desperately frightened to relinquish.

Thatch perceived himself as callow and ineffectual, never realizing that he was perceived by others in a much more accurate way: ingenious and forceful--and threatening to their precisely ordered world.

Milo Thatch suffered from a typically youthful combination of ardent zeal and a complete lack of confidence. Although it is true that the academic blowhards Thatch was interested in impressing found the lad to be an eccentric and an annoyance, young Thatch needn't have worried. As often happens, the greatest turning point in a life comes when least expected, and from a completely unknown quarter.

--P.B.W.

October 22, 1914

I surely began the day differently from how I have ended it. This morning I was filled with confidence in my ability, faith in my knowledge and research, and assured that my long-held goal was at last within reach. As I conclude the day, I am more weary, discouraged, and angry than I can ever remember being. The expedition of which I have dreamed will never take place. The study that has been of foremost importance in my life has gained no credibility. Years of effort within my occupation have proved fruitless. My resignation from the Cartography and Linguistics Department appears to have been enthusiastically accepted. I am also soaking wet.

The Board of Directors of the museum had finally granted an assembly to hear my proposal! For months, I had been carefully assembling the information for this presentation, cross-referencing my data, double-checking my conclusions, preparing charts, maps, and diagrams. I was ready. Every element of my presentation was succinct, supported, sound, and doggone it, essentially irrefutable!

There exists a book called the Shepherd's Journal, said to be a firsthand account of Atlantis and its exact whereabouts. Based on a centuries-old translation of a Norse text, the journal was long believed by historians to be in Ireland. But after comparing the text to the runes on a Viking shield in the museum's possession, I found that one of the letters had been mistranslated! By changing this letter and inserting the correct one, I found that the Shepherd's Journal, the very key to Atlantis, lies not in <u>Ireland</u> but in <u>Iceland</u>.

ᚨᛌᛚᚠᛇᛈ -ᚨᛌᛚᚠᛇᛈ

Coast of IRELAND

ᛐᚪᚠᚤᛌ ᚪᛈ -ᚨᛌᛚᚠᛇᛈ

Coast of ICELAND

That error having been corrected, to my mind my proposal to the Board was simplicity itself: It has long been held by authorities on the subject that Atlantis possessed a power source of some kind, more powerful than steam, coal, even our modern internal combustion engines. I proposed that we find Atlantis, find that power source, and bring it back to the surface.

In order to do so, to obtain the Shepherd's Journal was imperative. I had even plotted the route to take myself and a crew to the southern coast of Iceland to retrieve the Journal.

My interest in Atlantis and my enthusiasm for this specific field of study was not simply of intrinsic interest or importance. I must admit, a great deal of my passion for Atlantis is intensely personal, and can be traced directly to my grandpa, Thaddeus T. Thatch. It is a dream I had shared with him, and

Grandpa used to let me wear his helmet.

in many ways is a memorial to him, to his commitment, to the validity of his findings, and above all, to my respect and love for him. How fond I was of my grandpa, and how I miss him.

Just as I was departing my office for the presentation that I knew would change my professional standing and begin a whole new chapter of my life and work, I heard the familiar hiss and thump of a transit container arriving via pneumatic tube. This note was inside:

Dear Mr. Thatch: this is to inform you that your meeting today has been moved up from 4:30 pm to 3:30 pm.

                              --Harcourt

In a panic, I turned to the clock. My meeting moved to three-thirty? But it was already four o'clock! Just then, I again heard the sound of the message tube. A second note had arrived:

THEY CAN'T DO THIS TO ME!

I sped upstairs and into the main hall, where, I caught sight of Mr. Harcourt as he ran out of the museum and into his waiting automobile. He bellowed, "This museum funds scientific expeditions based on facts, not legends and folklore." Then he signaled to his chauffeur, who accelerated heedless of me.

I was so enraged by his lack of regard for my proposal, so desperate that he see the truth. I did what any rational person would do—I threatened to quit! I will never forget what Harcourt said next as long as I live: "You'll what? Flush your career down the toilet just like your grandfather?! You have a lot of potential, Milo. Don't throw it all away chasing fairy tales!"

A, I pack up my office I'm at a
loss for what to do now. Misery loves
company, and at least I have my
trusty cat Fluffy to go home to.

—M.J.T

October 22, 1914—Late Evening

A, I write this, I am being whisked away in the
dark of night, toward an unknown destination, in the
company of a total stranger.

When I got home this evening, Mrs. Jenkins in 209
asked me to come by and fix her radiator. Everybody
thinks I'm the building superintendant. Maybe they're
right. When I opened the door of my apartment, and
turned the light switch—no light. What now? I
turned the switch a few more times, to no avail.

A voice issued forth from the darkest quarter of my
ostensibly vacant rooms. "Milo James Thatch?" Since I
knew full well that my cat Fluffy doesn't talk, to say
that I was startled would be faint truth.

A flash of lightning illuminated the figure of a
beautiful blond woman against my parlor window. She
told me her name was **Helga Sinclair**. She
then informed me that her employer??? had a
"most intriguing proposition for me."

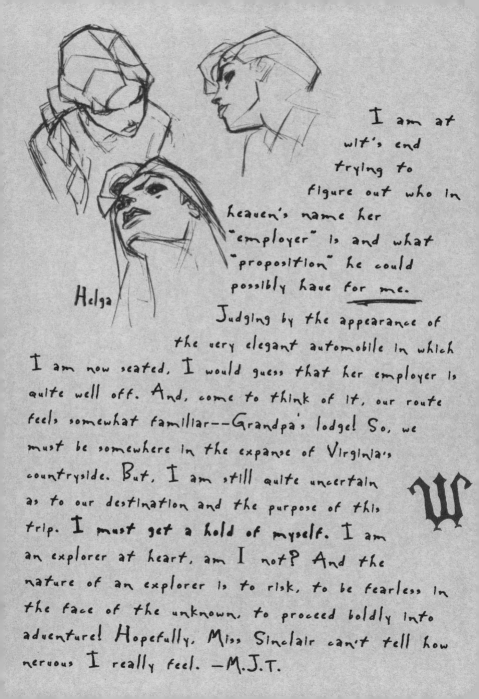

Helga

I am at
wit's end
trying to
figure out who in
heaven's name her
"employer" is and what
"proposition" he could
possibly have for me.

Judging by the appearance of
the very elegant automobile in which
I am now seated, I would guess that her employer is
quite well off. And, come to think of it, our route
feels somewhat familiar--Grandpa's lodge! So, we
must be somewhere in the expanse of Virginia's
countryside. But, I am still quite uncertain
as to our destination and the purpose of this
trip. I must get a hold of myself. I am
an explorer at heart, am I not? And the
nature of an explorer is to risk, to be fearless in
the face of the unknown, to proceed boldly into
adventure! Hopefully, Miss Sinclair can't tell how
nervous I really feel. —M.J.T.

October 23, 1924

I am living a waking dream! Since my last entry, my life has ascended from despair to a bliss beyond description. Perhaps if I record the remarkable events of last night, I can make sense of the remarkable journey I now find myself beginning.

Once we arrived at the foreboding house, Miss Sinclair led me inside and down a hallway into an elevator. I exited the elevator into a room filled with indescribable treasures from all over the world. I have never set eyes upon such an exquisite collection. If I didn't know better, I'd say I was in the British Museum. On one wall was an array of Assyrian sculptures, on another a sword that, if I didn't know better, I would say matched the description of Arthur's Excalibur. Timidly, I made my way down the hallway, but stopped abruptly when I noticed a large and impressive portrait on display. "Grandpa?"

"Finest explorer I ever met." I turned quickly. Seated on a pillow on the floor, practicing some contorting form of Eastern meditations was a strange, bearded, white-haired old man. From his peculiar pose, he offered not his hand, but his foot!

"Preston Whitmore. It's a pleasure to meet you, Milo." I stared at him, more than a bit bewildered.

This peculiar man told me that he and Grandpa had become close friends back in Georgetown, and that he had accompanied Grandpa on some of his expeditions.

Whitmore directed me to a package. And, while I was overcome to see that it was addressed in Grandpa's handwriting, I never could have hoped to discover what I did inside. The Shepherd's Journal!!! The key to finding the lost continent of Atlantis! Coordinates, clues...It was all before me.

I asked where it was found? Whitmore replied with a smile, "Iceland."

I KNEW IT!!!!

The book itself is fascinating. I have never seen such a binding. It is a rare example of the skill and craftsmanship of the ancient artisans. Beautiful on the outside, it has also dutifully preserved the treasure it keeps within!

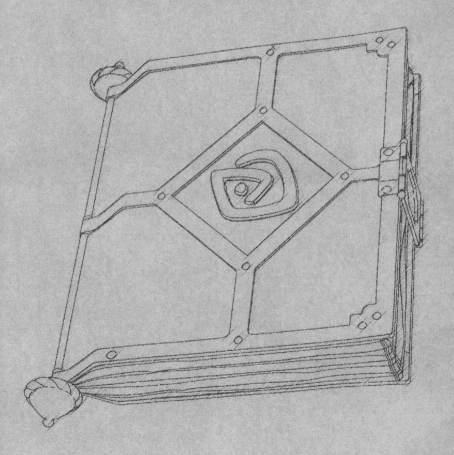

Whitmore makes good on his wager!!!

Whitmore explained to me that he made a bet with Grandpa that if Grandpa found the Shepherd's Journal, Whitmore would fund an expedition to Atlantis. Grandpa never said anything to me about his bet with Whitmore, but there was an evening at the Lodge in Virginia when I asked him how he intended to fund his research. He only said that money wouldn't be a worry. **It all makes sense now.**

As he told me this, Whitmore pushed a button and a table opened to reveal miniature models of an entire submarine expedition convoy, including a submarine boat, a digger, and even a dirigible!

Whitmore then spread out a pile of dossiers. He showed me photos and curriculum vitae of half a dozen of the best trained men and women—the same crew that brought the Journal back.

"All we need now is an expert in gibberish!

"Your granddad had a saying," Whitmore told me. "'Our lives are remembered by the gifts we leave our children.' That journal is his gift to you, Milo.

Atlantis is waiting."

The crew that brought the Shepherd's Journal back (front row): Manuel Ramirez, Mole, Rourke, Cookie; (back row): Vinny, Sweet, Grandpa, and Helga.

PART TWO

THE ULYSSES AND ITS CREW

An expedition sets sail, composed of a disparate group of fascinating mercenaries.

Although I had assembled a crack team for the Atlantis project, young Thatch wasn't simply an "expert in gibberish," as I so tactfully put it. I knew that if he was, as I expected him to be, an apple that had fallen close to his grandfather's tree, he would have passion, vision, and the right sense of proportion about the expedition that this olla podrida of a crew was about to embark upon. Perhaps I was being mysterious and melodramatic, perhaps I am as eccentric and barmy as people often tell me I am, but I needed to test my instincts about the lad, and he passed the test.

The following photo dossiers are the ones Thatch mentioned in his last entry. These are, in fact, the very items that I showed the astonished young fellow. I'll allow them to act as introduction to the members of the Atlantis expedition, and Thatch will fill in the rest. From this point in the lad's journal, there is little that I can add in terms of eyewitness insight, since I was eccentric and barmy enough to stay home--and let the experts do their jobs.

--P.B.W.

LYLE TIBERIUS ROURKE
Expedition Commander
Age: 54
Birthplace: Beaumont, Texas
Parents: Lt. Col. Jackson and

Expertise:
Joined U.S. Army in July 187[?]
Artillery Sgt. 1877. Fought at Wounded Knee
uprising 1890. Censured for use of excessive force
and refusal to acknowledge white flag of surrender.
Graduated second in class from West Point Academy,
1886. Tour of duty with Army Rough Riders, 1888-
1901. Wounded seven times in battle, commendation
for valor, commendation for saving the life of a
superior officer, commendation for leadership of C
Company under fire, censure for summary execution
of prisoners. Rose to rank of Captain on
battlefield of Spanish-American War. Ranked Expert
Marksman (awarded Golden Rifle four consecutive
years). Retired from Army 1901 to become
hand-to-hand combat instructor at Fort Dix,
Missouri. Also taught courses in survival tactics,
strategy, and chess. Began freelance career in May
1903 for British National Museum. Led expedition to
Valley of Kings in Egypt, 1903. Led return

pedition to Egypt, 1905. Led expedition to
Bolivia and Peru under Professor Thatch to retrieve
Idol of the Sun, 1906-08. Led expedition to
Antarctica 1909; credited with discovery and
destruction of lost city of Shub Nigruth. Led
expedition to Iceland to retrieve Shepherd's
Journal 1911. Currently on retainer.

Background:
Born the son of a Calvary Officer, Lyle T. Rourke
learned the transitory life of a military man at
an early age. Rourke Sr. was killed at Battle of
Spotsylvania, leaving behind his wife and only son,
Lyle. After repeated expulsions from boarding
school (fighting), Rourke determined to follow in
his fathers' footsteps and joined the military at
the age of fifteen by lying to his induction
officer about his age. Rourke exhibited a
remarkable talent for leadership, owing to his
analytical mind and charisma. He was married in
June of 1887, but his wife left him after only
four months of marriage. He does not make friends
easily. He is a pragmatist both personally and
professionally; he tends to take what he needs and
discards that which he considers "useless baggage."

HELGA KATRINA SINCLAIR
Age: 30
Birthplace: Frankfurt, Germany
Parents: Army Major Alexander Sinc   e

Expertise:
Miss Sinclair is skilled as a cool
instructor. She also possesses an analytical mind ideally
suited for strategy, tactics, or campaign planning. Her
charisma combined with her intelligence and aggressive
nature makes her an excellent trainer and enforcer. She is
the muscle behind Commander Rourke; when her commanding
officer issues an order, Miss Sinclair makes it her personal
business to see to it that everyone in her command follows
it to the letter. She is levelheaded in a crisis (see
attachment re: San Domingo 1904), and highly skilled in many
forms of small-arms combat; studied Aikido in Philippines
under Moreihei Ueshiba 1904-07, attaining rank of Yudansha-
Yondan. Expert in disciplines of Henka Waza, Tanto Dori and
Tachi Dori. Skilled in savate, tactical combat knife
fighting, Colt throwing knife, bo staff, kama, field tanto,
katana, as well as most conventional small arms. Has taught
rifle and shotgun at Quantico, Virginia, 1911. One of only
three (living) people to have bested Commander Rourke in
both unarmed combat and chess.

Background:

The oldest of six children (and the only girl), Miss
Sinclair grew up fighting with her fists as well as her
wits. Born in Frankfurt, Germany as the daughter of career
officer U.S. Army Major Alexander Sinclair. Extensive travel
at an early age, as well as exposure to a variety of
cultures and customs (Frankfurt 1884-87, Mannheim 1887-89,
Stuttgart 1889-92, Torii Station 1892, Vicenza 1892-93, Camp
Zama 1893-94, Yongsan 1894-97, Aberdeen Proving Ground,
1897-1901). Miss Sinclair exhibited exceptional athletic
skill at the age of four, and was encouraged by her mother
to pursue dance. Instead, with the influence of her father
and brothers, Miss Sinclair began learning the combat arts.
While stationed in Maryland at age seventeen, she was
introduced to Commander Rourke, and after relocating to Fort
Dix, began tactics and firearms training under him at the
behest of her father. Her skill impressed Commander Rourke,
as well as her potential (in Rourke's opinion) as a covert
agent and spy. She toured briefly with Commander Rourke,
acting as a training assistant, and then followed him in
1903 on expedition to Egypt as intelligence officer. Parted
company with Commander Rourke in August 1903 to continue
training. Married in 1907 to U.S. Army First Lieutenant
Christopher Jenkins. Presumed widowed 1908. First approached
by Whitmore Industries (at recommendation of Commander
Rourke) April 1911. Took position as bodyguard and chauffeur
for Preston Whitmore December 5, 1911. Currently employed in
aforementioned positions by Whitmore Industries.

JEBIDIAH ALLARDYCE FARNSWORTH
"COOKIE"
Age: 72
Birthplace: Tulsa, Oklahoma
Parents: Forsythe Ezekiel Farnsworth and Marianna Sweetwater

Expertise:
Despite his advancing years, "Cookie" Farnsworth remains at
the forefront in the area of field culinary preparation.
Farnsworth earned a reputation while enlisted in the U.S.
Army as a man who could literally feed legions with almost
no supplies at all. Renowned for his ability to find food or
supplies where there are seemingly none, regardless of
season, climate, or geography. Reputed to have prepared
lavish dinner for General Sheridan during Appomattox, that
centered around a dish said to be rabbit amandine, but was
in reality tomcat and bootsoles. "I heerd [sic] about this'n
from a Frenchman down Louisiana way." Experienced with
livestock, quartermastering, baking, and fur trapping. Did a
brief stint as a buffalo hunter in 1877.

Background:
Joined the 7th Michigan Cavalry Brigade under General
McLellan in 1861. Began work as a teamster and mule skinner.
Recruited as a sharpshooter by 2nd Lieutenant Colonel George
A. Custer. 3rd Division, Cavalry Corps, Army of the Potomac
in 1863 under General Pleasanton. Distinguished himself as
"Expert Marksman" at Battle of Chancellorsville. Promoted to

corporal. After spending a hungry week without supplies,
Farnsworth took it upon himself to begin training as a field
scout and cook. Showed remarkable aptitude as quartermaster,
but preferred the kitchen, "...it bein [sic] my true art an
all." Followed the newly promoted Brigadier General Custer
to the Michigan Cavalry Brigade; saw action at Gettysburg,
Bristoe, and Mine Run. Once again pressed into service as a
sharpshooter, Farnsworth is credited with shooting
Confederate General Pettigrew at Falling Waters in 1864.
After the War between the States, Farnsworth followed the
now demoted Lieutenant Colonel Custer as his personal chef
to Fort Laramie in Wyoming, 1866 with the 7th United States
Calvary. Toured with Custer during the 1867 Sioux and
Cheyenne Expedition. In May 1876, Farnsworth was blamed for
a rash of food poisoning that struck the entire officers
corps, and was demoted and transferred to the command of
general cook at Fort Abercrombie in North Dakota. Farnsworth
left the Army in 1878 and moved to Houston, Texas, where he
quickly rose to the position o;

Industries Stockyard and Feedl   ool
in Baton Rouge and New Orleans   rk
and opened Three Chestnut Rest   as
Chef. Sold restaurant at a los   on as
Chef for Waldorf Astoria Hotel   after
an altercation with a complair   words
concerning Farnsworths' expert   t in
the knee. Returned to work in
Industries as trail cook for   run.
Currently on retainer.

VINCENZO SANTORINI
Explosives and Demolitions
Age: 38
Birthplace: Palermo, Italy
Parents: Humberto and Fabiola San

Expertise:
Freelance Munitions and Ordinance
Mining 1900, Experience as Arson
Special consultant to Italia Bridge and Tunnel, 1903-04,
demolitions expert, Sicily Construction 1904, explosives
technician for Bentivegna Family Concrete and Olive Oil
Importers 1905, technical support and advisor to Addario
Meat Packing 1906, master's degree in engineering and
demolitions; Delphi Prison Correspondence Reform Program
1909, bachelor's degree in advanced chemistry, Delphi
Prison Correspondence Reform Program 1910, technical
overseer and hardrock blasting technician, Whitmore
Industries Mining 1913.

Background:
Vincenzo "Vinny" Santorini is the eldest child of
Humberto and Fabiola Santorini. The parents own and
operate a shop that specializes in floral arrangement and
holiday decorations. Because of an unfortunate, and to
date, unexplained explosion, the Santorini family was
forced to relocate their business. Young Vincenzo always

seemed to have a passion for and a fascination with
fire, and was disciplined often as a small boy for
lighting blazes. After the accident with the flower shop
in 1891, Vinny became more obsessed with pyrotechnics and
explosives. He began to mix his own formula for TNT in
1894 when he was eighteen. By the time he was twenty-
two, Vinny was known as an accomplished amateur chemist
who specialized in explosive compounds. It wasn't until
1899 that he was able to prove himself professionally in
the field as an explosives expert. He quickly grew in
reputation and fame as an authority on demolitions, and
garnered the attentions of local businessman Enrico
Bentivegna. While in the employ of the Bentivegna family,
Vinny seemed to drop from public sight. Clues as to his
whereabouts surfaced with the explosive destruction of
several delivery trucks of a business rival of Bentivegna.
It is known that Luca Addario approached Vinny about a
career change in late 1905. It is also known that Enrico
Bentivegna and four employees were killed in an explosion
that consumed their two automobiles. Italian authorities
were quick to place responsibility for the blast at the
feet of Vincenzo. He did a stretch of time in Milan's
Delphi Prison, where he continued his education as an
expert in the fields of engineering and demolitions. His
sentence was reduced by forty-two years in 1911.
Currently employed with Mining Division.

AUDREY ROCIO RAMIREZ
Chief Mechanic
Age: 18
Birthplace: Dearborn, Michigan
Parents: Manuel and Ana Ramirez

Expertise:
Began working in her father's   a
mechanic's assistant in 1901 a
early aptitude for mechanical engines; was promoted to
full apprentice at age of seven. Began work at Henry
Ford Automotive 1905 at age nine as journeyman mechanic.
Was given first supervisory position at age 11.
Instrumental in labor negotiations with fledgling
Automobile Workers Union, 1909. Credited with developing
prototype Assembly Line Production method, 1909.
Developed gear-driven centrifugal pump cooling system,
1910. Assisted in development of beveled drive gears,
1910. Assisted in development of Ford Reduction-Gear
Steering System (nonreversible) 1912.

Background:
The daughter of master mechanic Manuel Ramirez (retired
from Whitmore Industries) Audrey Rocio displayed
remarkable mechanical acuity from the time she could
first walk. At the age of eighteen months, she could
completely disassemble and reassemble any clock in the

Ramirez household. By the time Audrey was three, her
mother, Ana Ramirez, found that her daughter was able to
foil any lock she encountered. Mrs. Ramirez despaired of
trying to keep sweets in the house, as it became plain
that no matter how complex or expensive the pantry lock
was, Audrey could best it within minutes. Although nearly
as aggressive as her older sister Nena, Audrey was drawn
to the calm of her fathers' workshop. At the age of
four, Audrey rebuilt a '96 Quadracycle Runabout and it
became clear to Manuel that his daughter had what he
called "the touch." Although he could never tell his
paying customers that a toddler was repairing their
automobiles, Manuel took his daughter on as an apprentice.
In 1905, the Ramirez family moved to Detroit, where both
father and daughter took night jobs at the Henry Ford
Automotive Plant to supplement the income of Manuel's
shop. Audrey blossomed in the giant well-appointed
machine shop at Ford. She began a period of research and
invention, where she specialized in gear drives and
hydraulics. Her aggressive nature eventually put her in
the forefront of the new automotive labor movement. Henry
Ford, being a reasonable man, learned early on to take
Audrey Ramirez seriously. The Ford Motor Plant is now
recognized as one of the most enlightened and well-paying
manufacturers in the automobile industry. Manuel Ramirez,
upon his retirement, stated that only his daughter could
replace him, since he has never met a more gifted
mechanic. Currently on retainer.

JOSHUA STRONGBEAR SWEET
Medical Officer
Age: 42
Birthplace: Bigelowe, Kansas
Parents: Corporal Moses and Jerika Sweet

Expertise:
Ph.D. in Internal Medicine, Howard University, 1895;
Ph.D. in Botany, University of Maryland, 1896; Doctor
of Herbology, London 1897; first colored professor to
lecture at Harvard Medical School, 1897. Joined
military in 1898, toured with 1st United States
Volunteer Infantry (Rough Riders) until 1901, acting
as battlefield surgeon and Colonel Roosevelt's
personal physician for a period of three months
during the Kettle and San Juan Hill Campaigns. Was
instrumental in treatment of soldiers from both sides
of conflict in disease-ridden Cuban jungles after
hostilities had ceased. Received no formal
commendation except for personal letter from Colonel
Roosevelt. Has extensive knowledge of Arapaho and

Cheyenne healing techniques; mentored by his maternal
uncle, Iron Cloud. Traveled to India and studied
ayurvedic medicine at Amrita Institute, 1905. Traveled
to Ivory Coast and studied tropical medicine at Prins
Leopold Institute, 1908. Traveled to Tulsa, Oklahoma,
and studied large animal veterinary medicine at
Baxter University, 1913.

Background:
Born in an army clinic in Fort Phil-Kearny, Joshua
Sweet was raised by turns at Pine Ridge Reservation
in the Dakota Territory and various Army outposts
throughout Texas, Oklahoma, and Kansas. While living
on reservation territory, Dr. Sweet was tutored by
his uncle, an Arapaho elder and medicine man, Iron
Cloud. During this time, Dr. Sweet developed a talent
and appreciation for unconventional forms of medicine.
When living and traveling with the 24th Infantry, he
would assist the Medical Corps where his father was
assigned as a medic. Dr. Sweet is well-traveled and
well-versed in a wide variety of medical practices.
His background in botanical research and
pharmaceuticals is particularly useful when on
extended campaign. Dr. Sweet was first recruited by
then-Lieutenant Rourke after the battle of Santiago.
He is currently on retainer.

GAETAN MOLIERE
Mineralogist and Excavations
Age:39
Birthplace: Paris, France
Parents: Christophe and Gabrielle Moliere

Expertise:
Extensive knowledge of geology and pioneer in the
new science of tectonics. Advisor to Mining
National du France, Ottoman Mining, Australian
Opal Inc., New South Wales Coal, Slate and Granite
(Italy), and American Coal and Lumber. Has
developed or invented sixty-two independent mining
and excavation vehicles, tools, or related
equipment. Holds patents on fifty-nine of said
inventions. Acute senses, particularly taste and
smell, enable Moliere to correctly identify any
type of mineral or soil without benefit or aid of
any scientific apparatus 98.75% of the time.

Background:

Gaetan Moliere was born to a middle class working family, the youngest of four brothers. Both his parents were teachers; Christophe Moliere teaches university courses at the Sorbonne, and Gabrielle Moliere is a retired music teacher. Gaetan displayed an early interest in subterranean pursuits at age seven when he began exploring the vast sewer networks that lie underneath old Paris. By the age of thirteen, Moliere had developed a specialized type of goggles and headgear to wear while exploring caves in the surrounding countryside, as the sewers and catacombs held no further challenge or mysteries for him. He entered the Sorbonne at age seventeen, but left soon after when given the opportunity to act as special technical advisor to a local mining company. Soon thereafter, Moliere developed ███████ ███████████████████████████████ of the █████████ ██████ and identify ██████ ████ soils. ███ ██ sensitive to t█████████████████████ y ████████ ████ e does not █████████████████████████ r█████ throwing a███████████████████ is to ████████████ insects.

WILHELMINA BERTHA PACKARD
Communications Officer
Age: 61
Birthplace: Whippany, New Jers
Parents: Lionel and Claudette

Expertise:

Wilhelmina Packard (Mrs.) Research assistant and
reputed mistress of Dr. Mahlon Loomis from July to
November of 1875. Developed the galvanometer, and
with the help of Dr. Loomis, the concept of Hertzian
wave application. Worked as research assistant and
eventually as a full partner to Dr. Nathan
Stubblefield, developing the vibrating telephone in
1888. Married Dr. Stubblefield, 1891. Secured
congressional appropriation of $50,000 for further
development of work. Appropriation was never
forthcoming, for reasons known only to Congress.
Divorced Dr. Stubblefield, 1893. Traveled and worked
with Guglielmo Marconi, 1898-1901. Instrumental in
December transatlantic broadcast. Worked as research
fellow for Victor Talking Machine, 1902-04. Developed
sodion nonregenerative detector, 1902. Developed
bornite movable cup perkion detector, 1903. Worked
for Atwater-Kent 1904-07. Helped develop radak type

R-4 regenerative circuit and holds sole patent for
the orthosonic circuit. Worked for Magnavox 1907-12.
Developed AC-3-C Battery.

Background:
The daughter of traveling performers, Wilhelmina
Packard grew up on the road. At the age of sixteen,
she joined the Flora Dora Girls. Toured for two
seasons as an exotic dancer. First documented
marriage to U.S. Calvary Officer Dennis Whitehead
June, 1870. Widowed February, 1871. Married to
Pennsylvania State Representative Grover Truman, May
1871. Rep. Truman arrested for bigamy June 1871;
marriage annulled. While Mrs. Packard worked variously
as waitress, dance-hall girl, and seamstress, her
interests began to take her into the newfangled field
of electronic communication devices. After the Dr.
Loomis affair, she married no fewer than six husbands
between 1876 and 1890. After Dr. Stubblefield, Mrs.
Packard again married, this time to Chichester Bell,
cousin of Alexander Graham Bell, 1893. Divorced later
the same year. Mrs. Packard met her most recent
husband while at the Bell Aerial Experiment
Association in 1907. Curtis Packard coupled a passion
for electronic communication with the notion of
heavier-than-air flight. Mrs. Packard widowed in 1912.
Currently on retainer as research and development
chief for Communications Division.

October 24, 1924

Everything is moving so quickly. My possessions have been put in storage, my resignation from the museum (truly) delivered. All the details of my departure appear to have been attended to by Mr. Whitmore in advance. Naturally, the haste of my egress dictated a certain degree of trust in the odd old fellow, but I felt a bit better after I was able to get a little information on my eccentric benefactor, from the 1923 City Directory.

Must glue Whitmore Care Instructions for Fluffy:
- Likes to be scratched behind her ears
- Prefers buttermilk
- Allergic to albacore!
- Enjoys learning about languages and cultures
- Particularly adept at acting as bookmark

PRESTON B. WHITMORE

Mr. Preston Whitmore is the founder and sole owner of Preston Whitmore Industries, Ltd., an empire that encompasses logging operations in the states of Washington and Oregon; the Southern Rail Freight Line; Whitmore Mining and Petroleum in Texas, Alaska Territories, and South Africa; Whitmore Stockyards in Houston, Texas; and P.W.I. Shipbuilding in Norfolk, Virginia. An avid collector of rare antiquities, Mr. Whitmore has spent sizeable fortunes on expeditions to retrieve precious relics, with the help of his longtime friend and advisor Prof. Thaddeus Thatch.

IRV
Mr.
four
ama
Mo
enc
in
an
Ra
M
m
S
S
a
V
a

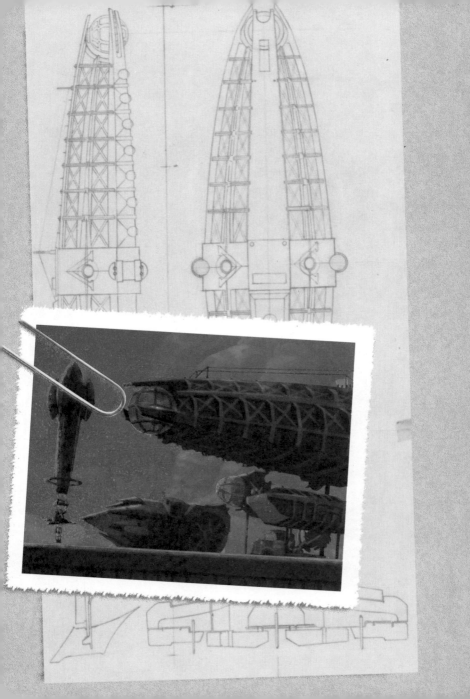

Some notes about the giant
submarine boat Ulysses:

- Hide is made of thick metal, riveted
  into a sleek skin.

- a pair of large propellers astern and a
  colossal aft rudder.

- atop the vessel, a large gun turret
  perched with two smaller turrets, one on
  each side—each built to move a full 360
  degrees)

- bottom of ship—rigged with two rows of
  capsules that contained smaller
  submarine vessels.

- front of the ship has gyroscopic
  bathysphere with decks on three levels,
  including the bridge.

  - hidden inside belly of cover ship
  Lewis & Clark presumably launched
  from Norfolk Shipping Yards

A remarkable feat of engineering!

Crew members

The first crew member I met was **Vinny Santorini**, the expedition demolitions expert. Almost ran me over with his "Office supplies."

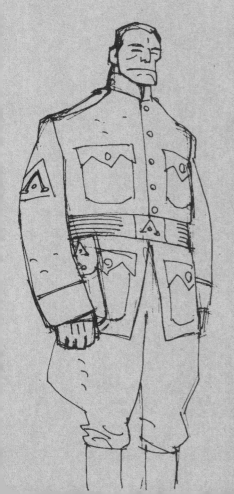

Whitmore introduced me to **Commander Rourke** — the man Grandpa trusted to lead the Iceland team that brought the Journal back.

Have to go now...

October 24, 1914, Evening

This first night of our voyage finds me short on sleep, but with no deficit of enthusiasm about our mission. I would do well to get a good night's rest. Whitmore's parting words echo through my mind—"Make us proud, boy!"

I've claimed a berth for myself and I'm settling in just fine. This afternoon's unpleasant introduction to Molière (AKA Mole)

MOLE

notwithstanding, I find my interactions with the crew have all been without incident. I must admit, however, that I have tended to hang back and observe until now.

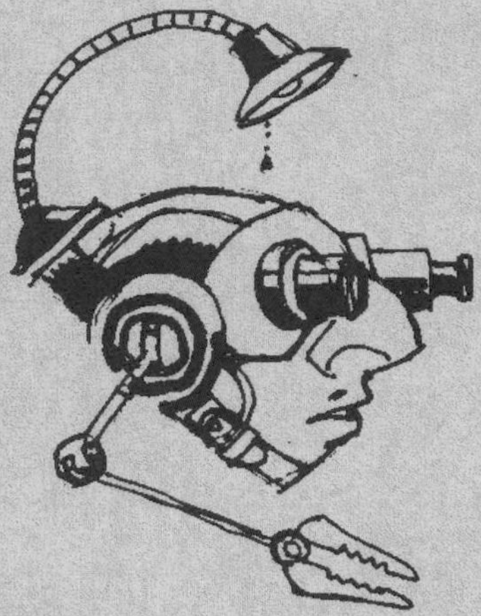

The Leviathan I saw was the guardian to the portal of Atlantis! His eyes glowed red. His body was as long as twenty ships. His tail was like the tail of a fish. His arms were like the arms of a crab.

Tomorrow is the day that I am to address the assembled crew. It will be my familiarization presentation for the rest of the expedition team. I am a little nervous but I've prepared magic lantern slides to illustrate my presentation. The first slide is of the Leviathan. So, my points are as follows:

- Legend has it the Leviathan was a creature so frightening that sailors were said to have been driven mad by the mere sight of it.

- The creature is described in the book of Job (41.1, to be exact). The Bible says, "Out of his mouth go burning lights, sparks of fire shoot out."

- We need to be on the lookout for a carving or a sculpture created to frighten the superstitious.

- According to the Shepherd's Journal, the path to Atlantis will take us down a tunnel at the bottom of the ocean. We will come up a curve into an air pocket, where the remnants of an ancient highway will lead us to Atlantis. The arrangement of the whole thing is akin to the grease trap in a sink. One thing bothers me. How did the shepherd know of this vast underwater world? There is only one explanation, a theory that expedition geologist Moliere confirmed to me today. In the shepherd's time, the earth was experiencing a global ice age, which lowered sea levels around the globe. This, with the normal movement of the tectonic plates, would suggest that in the shepherd's time, Atlantis was above ground. This further suggests that the Leviathan may have even been a flying vehicle at one time.

October 25, 1914

~~I can't believe what happened~~ ~~day~~ ~~that happened~~ ~~to us.~~??

I struggle to pen this entry and to digest what has happened to us. The frayed vestiges of our crew are now regrouping, trying to assess our status and our future.

Seven hours ago, we were 200 strong. Now, I don't know who's left, all I know is that we aren't many. We should have been aware of the danger when we came to the graveyard of lost ships—scattered as far as the eye could see over the ocean floor beneath us, there appeared to be shipwrecked vessels from every era in maritime history.

I was so engrossed in consulting the Shepherd's Journal, so focused on finding our path, that I misinterpreted what I was reading and failed to take heed of the Journal's warnings. I translated from the Journal,

"⟨ᘔ⟩⟨ᘔ⟩⟨ᘔ⟩ ⟨ᘔ⟩⟨ᘔ⟩ ⟨ᘔ⟩⟨ᘔ⟩⟨ᘔ⟩⟨ᘔ⟩ ⟨ᘔ⟩⟨ᘔ⟩ ⟨ᘔ⟩⟨ᘔ⟩⟨ᘔ⟩⟨ᘔ⟩⟨ᘔ⟩
⟨ᘔ⟩⟨ᘔ⟩⟨ᘔ⟩ ⟨ᘔ⟩⟨ᘔ⟩ ⟨ᘔ⟩⟨ᘔ⟩ ⟨ᘔ⟩⟨ᘔ⟩⟨ᘔ⟩⟨ᘔ⟩⟨ᘔ⟩ ⟨ᘔ⟩⟨ᘔ⟩⟨ᘔ⟩ ⟨ᘔ⟩⟨ᘔ⟩

⟨ᘔ⟩⟨ᘔ⟩⟨ᘔ⟩ ⟨ᘔ⟩⟨ᘔ⟩ ⟨ᘔ⟩⟨ᘔ⟩⟨ᘔ⟩⟨ᘔ⟩ ⟨ᘔ⟩⟨ᘔ⟩⟨ᘔ⟩ ⟨ᘔ⟩⟨ᘔ⟩ ⟨ᘔ⟩⟨ᘔ⟩⟨ᘔ⟩
⟨ᘔ⟩⟨ᘔ⟩ ⟨ᘔ⟩ ⟨ᘔ⟩⟨ᘔ⟩⟨ᘔ⟩⟨ᘔ⟩⟨ᘔ⟩⟨ᘔ⟩

"Enter the lair of the Leviathan, last of the mighty war gods. There you will find the path to the gateway."

It started when Packard heard a strange sound

coming through the hydrophone. Then suddenly, the entire vessel was rocked with a percussive impact! Through the glass of the bathysphere we saw it! **The Leviathan itself!** The enormous lobster—shaped creature reared back and prepared to strike at the Ulysses with its massive claw.

On board—pandemonium! The Leviathan grabbed the Ulysses with its mighty claws. Its giant eye glared menacingly through the glass.

Observing from such close range, <u>I was startled to discover that the **Leviathan was a machine!**</u>

It began to crush the Ulysses. Subpods manned with crew members ejected from the launching docks and quickly grouped to attack the Leviathan. Their torpedoes seemed to break the hold of the mighty machine.

As two of the turrets swiftly turned to fire on the Leviathan the great machine turned and discharged what I can only describe as a beam of pure electricity. The beam shattered into the Ulysses and blew a hole right through her!

Water flooded into the ship. The outside pressure fractured metal plates and sent rivets shooting from the ship's seams.

We needed to evacuate!

two sets of claws

underbelly reveals the
Leviathan's mechanical
nature

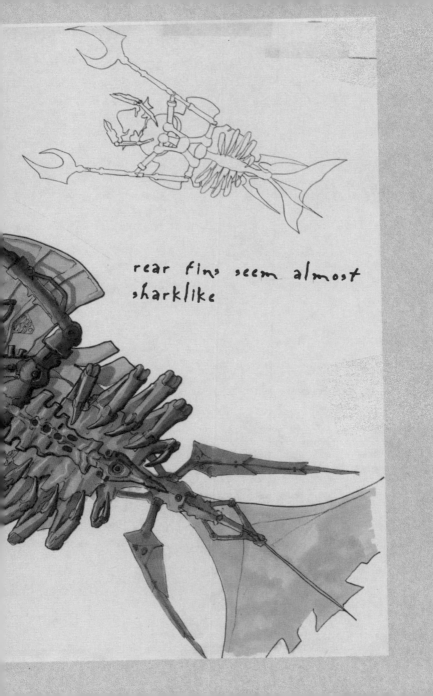

rear fins seem almost
sharklike

The crew rushed to the aqua evac vehicles and blasted from the dying submarine just as the Leviathan crushed the Ulysses into memory.

After my first blundering, I desperately tried to maintain focus. According to the Shepherd's Journal we were looking for a big crevice. Sighting a likely looking fissure nearby while dodging the falling debris of the Ulysses, what was left of her crew, made their way into the opening.

The Leviathan was unable to follow the escape vehicles into the narrow crevice. It discharged another deadly electrical beam that hit one of the subpods. The damaged vessel collided directly with an escape vehicle, which crashed into the cave wall. My heart pounded as we made our way.

Our single remaining aqua evac and one subpod, manned by Vinny and Mole, made their way through the submerged cave. Reaching an air pocket, we surfaced in a gloomy underground grotto.

Rourke is calling us together. —M.J.T.

PART THREE
A PERILOUS JOURNEY

The expedition follows an ancient highway, their
path punctuated with dangerous challenges and
imposing obstacles.

Exploration is by its very nature a path fraught
with peril, and often death. Whether it is a
Bolivian jungle, an Arctic waste, the caverns of
Mammoth Caves, or the newfangled subway system of
New York City, all journeys born of curiosity have
unexpected and often hazardous results.

Did the expedition crew assembled for this
journey know of the dangers that awaited them? Of
course they did. But still, few people truly begin
a day with the realization that it could be their
last. The loss of so many valiant men and women and
the disaster of the Ulysses causes me pain and
remorse to this day and probably will for the rest
of my years. There is, sadly, always a price to be
paid for discovery.

My great consolation is that every one of the
Ulysses crew knew the potential consequences--both of
danger and of glory--that awaited

them on their voyage. Much like the crew of
Captain Nemo's famous Nautilus, they had "a
plan for living, but also a plan for dying."

The stupendous findings that resulted from
continuing the expedition after the Leviathan
disaster are a fitting memorial to the courage
of the entire expedition crew, including those
who did not return.

--P.B.W.

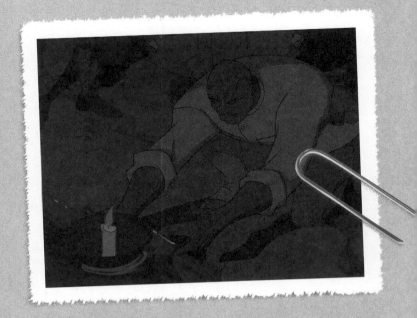

October 26, 1914

We're a smaller and more humble body.
with a greater sense of the real mystery and
danger that await us. As we regrouped, Dr.
Sweet led a modest memorial, placing a candle
in an upturned helmet and floating its faint
light of honor, over the water and into the
engulfing darkness. We paid a hushed tribute to
our fallen comrades.

Commander Rourke, sensing the need for veneration and a demand for the reassembly of our mission, gave a brief encouragement. He finished with a dreadful command to me. "It looks like our chances for survival rest with you and that little book, Mr. Thatch."

The searchlight from the aqua evac revealed the gloomy surroundings of the cave where we found ourselves. The defining feature of our location was a giant carved dragon's head at an entrance or egress. The dragon's head appeared to be the beginning of some kind of Atlantean roadway, and with Rourke's encouraging words, the remaining crew burst into a heartening flurry of consolidated activity to begin a journey into the dragon's mouth.

Miss Sinclair assembled everyone to stations. Mole on point, Audrey on the oiler. Everyone listened intently and responded quickly. I waited nervously because I knew now that I was being relied upon, and I did not want to disappoint my colleagues. I was assigned to drive a truck, and gamely tried to bluff my experience in vehicle operation, which at that point was limited to a bumper car at Coney Island—which certainly runs on the same basic principles!

Suffice it to say that an academic understanding is often a pale inferior to experience, and the truck in my charge was soon being towed behind the digger.
—M.J.T.

The carved Dragon's head

Keeping track of the date in this subterranean locale seems an exercise in futility and triviality.

A forbidding cave confronted our crew. The structure was shaped like a huge skull; each grotto entrance resembled the eye socket of the skull. Studying the Journal, I directed the crew to one of the caverns. As the crew began their entry to the cave, they quickly retreated, as a fearsome subterranean monster leapt out after them!

I am afraid that I am not dealing very well with the responsibility Rourke has laid upon me. I realized that in my haste to provide direction, I had been reading the Shepherd's Journal upside down. Knowing that the lives of the crewmembers rest in my hands is, at times, unbearable.

These cumulative blunders have not endeared me to the rest of the crew. It seems the harder I try, the more I am inclined to stumble, and over the past few days I have wearily accepted the status of "official expedition dunderhead."

Grandpa told me once, "Don't worry about people who kid you. If they didn't like you, they wouldn't spend the effort — they'd just ignore you."

—M.J.T.

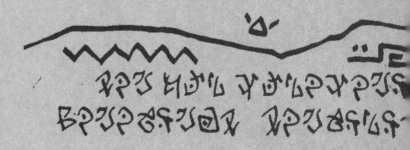

And the path went on and I walked. And I saw giant columns like

I remain a figure of fun for the rest of the group, who see no harm in leveling at me a series of practical jokes and derisive mockery that make me feel more and more dispirited with each prank. Worse, as my worth to the expedition lessens in the eyes of my comrades, I begin to be outcast and ignored. I remember my grandfather's admonition, and begin to worry that I am essentially worthless to the expedition.

For instance, the crew has taken to assembling around a fire to eat together. I sit yards away, not noticed and not included, writing these entries and studying the Shepherd's Journal.

—M.J.T.

giant trees that grew in the dark underground forest of stone.

before

Our path was obstructed by a giant stone pillar. It was at least half a mile high, and its elaborate engineering, construction, and decoration must have taken hundreds— perhaps thousands—of years.

As I marveled at this magnificent antiquity, Vinny pulled me away and nonchalantly blew up the column's base, causing it to collapse horizontally in a cloud of ancient dust and modern smoke.

What are we doing here???

—M.J.T.

and after . . . the destruction of a priceless treasure in the quest for survival.

I finally got to be of some use to this expedition. Our convoy was stopped in front of a large wall that blocked our progress.

Vinny was evidently disappointed to find that his depleted cache of explosives simply wasn't enough to break through the impediment, and Commander Rourke determined that our only alternative was to dig.

Mole, whose excavation skills had been hitherto unused on this expedition, was overjoyed at the prospect of burrowing through the barrier. He cackled and growled delightedly in his peculiar French prattle at the obstruction before him, and soon had the engine of the digger roaring. He had barely begun to bore through the wall when the digger shorted out and the cabin filled with smoke, stalled, and stopped with a mechanical groan. Thwarted on the pathway to delight, Mole banged his head on the steering wheel in despair.

I am in constant awe of the fleet of vehicles Whitmore has assembled—all to settle a bet with Thaddeus!

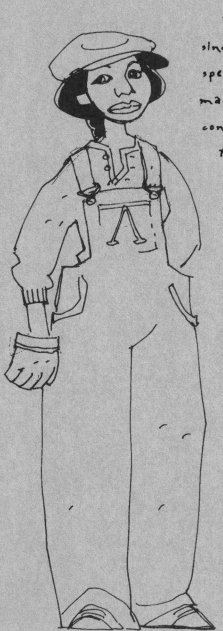

AUDREY was perplexed since her morning had been spent fine-tuning the digging machine. I recognized the contraption's dying groan as that of an HV (same as the museum basement's boiler). I approached Audrey as she opened the digger's engine door. She determined (incorrectly) that the problem stemmed from a faulty rotor, and set off for a spare from one of the trucks.

I waited for Audrey to leave and then quickly set upon the errant motor, finally gluing it a healthy blow with a handy wrench. As I had suspected, it immediately

Mrs. Packard took this photo of me in the act

coughed back to life! We could get on our way. Then
Audrey swung her fist as if to punch my arm but
stopped. I recoiled. "Two for flinching," she grinned as
she then punched me twice in the arm—hard—and then
walked away. As I rubbed my soon-bruised arm, I could
hear Mole cackling in the background.

I recognized again that academic
understanding is often a pale inferior to
real experience.

They're not ignoring me. Grandpa—M.J.T.

Our convoy stopped to make camp for the "night" at the edge of a bridge. The attention of the whole crew was drawn to a rock formation hanging from the cave roof. The formation glowed with an eerie luminescence. We all stood mesmerized, and tried to ascertain what was causing the glow.

Here I am "leading" the way.

I consulted the Journal in search of a clue about this magnificent object. I discovered a drawing, but any explanation of the glow appears to have been torn from the book's binding.

Perhaps out of boredom, or perhaps in a genuine effort to break down the wall between us, Audrey and Dr. Sweet pulled me into conversation about the Shepherd's Journal. They were curious about the book's contents and about the amount of time I was expending studying it.

I explained that I was having a problem making sense of some of it. In one passage, the Shepherd seems to be leading up to something called "the Heart of Atlantis." I thought it might be the power source the legends refer to. But then the text just cuts off, almost as if there is a page missing.

All of them looked at me quizzically. Vinny suggested I relax, and joked that, "We don't get paid overtime."

I know that sometimes I get a little carried away but I was shocked to find the crew did not share my enthusiasm. I thought that we were all in it for the discovery, the teamwork, the adventure. I was disappointed when the crew revealed that they were, in fact, in it for the money. Why did I not see that coming?

Later that night, I was half-asleep, when the call of nature summoned me from my tent. I walked past Cookie, who mumbled in his sleep, "Redhead's got a gun." I still have no idea what this means.

As I...tended to business, I inadvertently shined my portable torch at the phosphorescent rock "chandelier" high above the cavern. The faint beam appeared to awaken what seemed to be a cluster of small glowing fireflies. I was bewitched by the beauty of the glowing insects, as they gracefully descended through the darkness and toward the camp. But as these peculiar flies landed on the canvases of the tents and vehicles, they burst into flames! The fireflies swarmed and seemed to attack the camp. The conflagration leapt from tent to tent, and in a matter of seconds the entire encampment was ablaze.

I screamed "FIRE!" at the top of my lungs, and soon the entire camp was a farrago of fire, smoke, and pandemonium.

My memory of the events that follow is a bit vague, and someday I will ask my colleagues exactly what transpired. I know that Rourke saw that there was no use fighting the blaze, and ordered Miss Sinclair to gather the expedition crew together and under cover in the nearby trees.

Chaos reigned. The sound of the inferno (and soon, the explosions) was deafening, as everyone ran helter-skelter toward their various tasks. Cookie cracked his whip at his electric mule. The convoy quickly started over the bridge. Pelted by a swarm of fireflies, a fuel truck ignited and exploded, breaking the bridge in two. The Digger began to

All of them look
I relax, and joked t
   I know that so
but I was shocked
enthusiasm. I tho'
the discovery, t
was disappointed
they were
di

Firefly

,lide backward, forcing the rest of the convoy
down with it. Mole frantically tried to
switch gears, but to no avail. The trucks
disappeared down the crumpled bridge into
the dark chasm below.
   At some point in the thunderous carnage
         of our chaotic escape, everything
         around me went black.
              —M.J. T.

 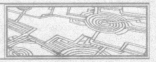
PART FOUR
A DRAMATIC ADVENTURE

A breathtaking tour of the ancient city, and the
confidence of a royal princess.

I knew that young Thatch would bring his scholarly
intelligence and myriad academic skills to this
expedition. I also knew that he would bring a fierce
determination, passion, and joy of discovery to the
team, qualities that I had hoped would influence and
inform the rest of the expedition and its members. I
knew that Thatch Junior had the same tenacious vision
as his pesky granddad. If I knew anything at all, it
was that he was the right man for the job, and a good
kid to boot.

What I hadn't considered was the converse. I
hadn't contemplated the influence that might be
wrought on the lad from the expedition and its crew
--for his personal good or ill. And if Thatch hadn't
had the same strength of character that had made
Thaddeus such a good man and good friend, he would
not have survived to the point where we find him now.
As I read his writings, I sense the passage of
naiveté to maturity, of academia to experience, of
fine lad to fine man.

But following the discovery of Atlantis and its inhabitants, the shoe was well and truly on the other foot. Thatch, the erstwhile fish out of water, had found an ocean of opportunity. Where once he had felt worthless and outcast, now he was not only important to the mission, but without his knowledge, intelligence and cultural diplomacy, everyone else was doomed. In essence, whether he knew it or not, Thatch was being thrust into the position of leader.

The others in the expedition were the outsiders now, ignorant of the language, oblivious of the culture, and each carrying with them, to varying degrees, a dangerous attitude of cultural superiority. (It's often wise, no matter how right you are, to keep your trap shut.)

I'm just doggone sorry old Thaddeus couldn't be present to witness that metamorphosis, but I'm gratified that said evolution is conspicuous between the lines of Milo's own account.

Oh, yes. One more thing. Young Milo was the only one of the expedition who had an Atlantean princess who thought that he was worthy of her attentions.

--P.B.W.

Atlantis Lives!!!

Atlantis is literally alive.

It's like walking into the ruins of Troy or Ephesus and finding the streets teaming with Trojans or Ephesians. It is not the dusty archaeological ruin I expected but a place, a real city, a community. The exquisite architecture and beautiful materials of the buildings, the strange and exotic flora, the very vibrant energy and most importantly the people. Especially Kida. (But more about her later.) Though the discovery of a living, breathing population is exhilarating, it is not without serious complications.

the King

I've just returned from the palace of the king of Atlantis and I am deeply concerned. Rourke took the lead and spoke with great bravado and arrogance that visibly angered the king (an imposing figure) who understandably felt threatened by our presence.

I must confess, although I had admired his leadership and efficiency, Commander Rourke's patronizing and domineering attitude disturbed me greatly.

When Rourke protested that we were peaceful explorers and men of science, the king naturally pointed out the expedition's weapons.

Although Rourke nimbly attempted to explain the armaments, the king was having none of the commander's rationale, and ordered us to return to our people and leave Atlantis at once.

The King at last consented to Rourke's request that we be allowed to stay the night, to rest, re-supply, and make ready to travel by morning.

A bit about Kida.

Kida, the king's daughter, was the first Atlantean I encountered. She bears the markings and attire of a warrior and wears a crystal around her neck. It turns out that all the Atlanteans wear a similar crystal.

Have I mentioned Kida is quite beautiful? I was able to observe her at length during our visit with the king and when she returned my gaze it sent a jolt right through me and I felt an unsettling combination of fellowship and fear. I think it's called chemistry. I sense that she and her father do not see eye to eye on all matters—in particular, the presence of our group.

Obviously I (and the rest of the crew) want to know so much more about Atlantis and its people. So without much time left to us by the king's order to leave, it was agreed that I would set out to find Kida and discover more about this remarkable world.

One additional thought: My knowledge of the Atlantean language has made me the only indispensable member of the team — a concept that would have seemed unfathomable when we set out.

—M.J.T.

I set off for the king's chambers. I saw Kida leaving, and watched her from the column I was hiding behind. To be honest, I was nervous and a little afraid, and had to give myself a little "pep talk."

As I formulated my questions and steeled myself to make an intractable demand for information from Kida, the princess surprised me from behind and clamped her royal hand over my mouth. She pushed aside a large stone, revealing the entrance to an overgrown cave filled with an odd assortment of tools, artifacts, statues, and other objects.

Kida was interested in finding out about my world. She had surmised that I was a scholar. The way she had deduced this, however, was a blow to my self-confidence.

fisherman

She said that judging from my "diminished physique and large forehead" I am suited for nothing else. Ouch!

In her excitement and enthusiasm, Kida collided questions one into the next. In order to avoid an academic train wreck, I suggested a round-robin.

The Atlanteans sure have some strange vehicles.

Here's what she revealed:

—The gods became jealous.

—A great cataclysm
banished the empire.

—The sky went dark.

—A bright light, like a star,
floated about the city.

—Kida believed light called
her mother to it.

—She never saw her mother again.

Note: When I claimed that it seemed
impossible that she could remember
the details of this catastrophic event
because it would make her something
like 8,500 years old, she benignly
confirmed her age.

Jiminy Christmas!

Kida then asked how it was that I found my way here.

I showed her the Shepherd's Journal and explained that it was this book that held the key to our expedition. She turned the Journal over and over in her hands, running her fingers over the pages, and examining it with great astonishment.

She asked if I could understand the contents of the Journal. Her expression following my affirmative response revealed to me that she could not read. She could not understand her own written language!?!

She explained sheepishly that such knowledge had been lost to the Atlanteans since the time of the MEH-behl-moak (the Great Flood).

The princess asked me to read from the Shepherd's Journal. "LEH-weg-tem SHEE-buhn puhk BEN-tem DEE-gen-mil SAH-tib. Yoos KEH-ruhn-tem SHAHD-luhg KOAM-tib-loh-nen."
"Follow the narrow passage for another league. There, you will find the fifth marker."

She promptly informed me that my Atlantean accent was boorish and provincial, and that I spoke the language through my nose (I'll have to work on that). But she seemed genuinely exhilarated by my ability, and I could sense a continuing lessening of her misgivings about me. In fact, I could sense in her, and I believe she in me, a kindred spirit.

She led me to a giant, exquisitely detailed and decorative stone fish which appeared to be some sort of vehicle. Kida confirmed that it was indeed a vehicle, but confessed that after many attempts, she could not actuate the machine's motive power. I studied the writings carved on this remarkable "fish."

Kida and I worked together: I decifered the instructions and the princess used that remarkable crystal as a "key." After a few false starts, a burst of blue-hued energy from within it lighted the vehicle's surface, and with a slight shudder, the remarkable machine began to hover.

The strange "flying bicycle" was operational, but only for an instant. For reasons that are unknown to me, the vehicle gave out. (I hope Whitmore purchased traveler's insurance for the crew.)

We set out on a tour of her amazing city. Together we scaled a giant stone statue, covered with centuries worth of overgrowth. As we reached the top, Kida's magnificent metropolis was spread out at our feet.

The events of the day, the discoveries, the fulfilled hopes and answered prayers, all culminated for me at that moment, and I was overwhelmed. As I wiped a tear from my eye, Kida asked me what was wrong.

In what I assumed was a courageous and manly fashion, I blamed my tears on a foreign object irritating my eye. One look at Kida showed me that she didn't trust my answer.

And, that I could absolutely trust her with the honest truth.

So, I told her what had really moved me to tears. I explained how Grandpa had told me stories of this place as far back as I could remember. And that I just wished he could be here with me now. Kida's soft smile eased my pang.

Typical Atlantean architecture. Stone construction.

The city of Atlantis is a spectacular ruin. There appears to be almost no "new" construction, all is in a state of magnificent decay.

Atlantian Boat

During our wanderings, we stopped outside an Atlantean establishment that in certain seacoast cities back home would be called a "tattoo parlor."

Kida explained that the ritual branding of complex inked designs was an integral part of the Atlantean culture. As among some of the tribes native to New Zealand, the number and arrangement of these permanent skin decorations was determined by physical, intellectual, artistic, or cultural achievement. The hierarchy and explication of these emblematic citations appeared rich and complex, and I hope to be able to study it further one day.

We wandered the marketplaces. At a booth, Kida gave an Atlantean some currency. In return, he gave each of us a stick with some sort of tentacled creature on it. I was somewhat bewildered, not knowing what I was expected to do with such an object, when Kida demonstrated—she began to eat the poor creature's tentacles.

Well, no need to appear provincial! (It was rather delicious. Reminiscent of chicken.)

Now I find myself at the close of what has been the best day of my life. Kida has treated me to an authentic **Atlantean** dinner. I sit here happily examining every oddly-shaped dinner utensil, partaking of every unusual foodstuff, surrounded by Atlanteans, enjoying their mundane (to them, but not to me) conversations. —M.J.T.

Two elder atlantean gentlemen in characteristic dress. Drawn outside the tattoo parlor.

 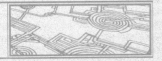
PART FIVE
A DEVASTATING BETRAYAL
An insidious and shocking plan
for pillage and profit.

Greed. I have never really understood it. I
have worked like a dog to get everything I
have, and have always found plain old greed
a sign of laziness or ignorance, or both.
None of the wealth I have acquired or the
industry I have built would mean two hoots
to me if I had just taken it. The pleasure
has been in the earning of it, and that
provides a pleasure that goes on and on.

Young Thatch hadn't a greedy bone in his
being. He was most sincere in his
appreciation of discovery, teamwork, and
adventure. The wealth he sought on this
expedition was historical, intellectual, and
chiefly philosophical. It was personally
enriching to the lad, to be sure, but Milo

didn't care a bit about crossing his palm
with silver--unless it happened to be an
archaeological artifact made of that
precious metal.

As I have said, this was an expedition
of personal discovery and growth for Thatch,
and his evolution along the path of this
journey to this point, as he has so far
indicated in his own words, had been
remarkable.

Now, he was about to discover the
qualities that separate ordinary men from
heroes.

--P.B.W.

WHIRLWIND.

The word never had such meaning. The episodes that followed my wonderful time with Kida were so overwhelming. I'll attempt to recapture the highlight (many more aptly described as lowlights).

I have discovered the heart of Atlantis.

After our repast, Kida led me to an underwater pool. She asked me to follow in order to show me an underwater mural that I could see at first glance depicted many milestones in the history of Atlantis.

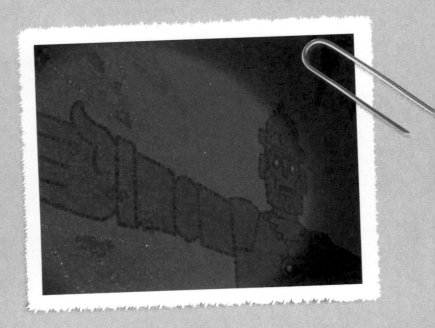

I used the crystal that now glowed around Kida's neck to illuminate the wall. One particular drawing was of a large blue crystal that had fallen from the sky. Another depicted Atlanteans wearing small pieces of the same blue crystal around their necks. It was then I saw the light. Literally. This was the heart of Atlantis! That's what the Shepherd Aziz was talking about! It wasn't a star, it was a crystal, like the crystal around Kida's neck! The power source I had been looking for and the bright light Kida remembered from her distant childhood!

They were the same thing!

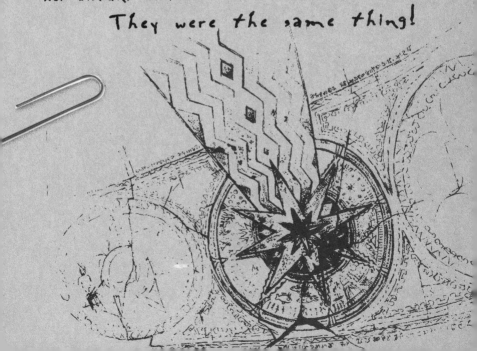

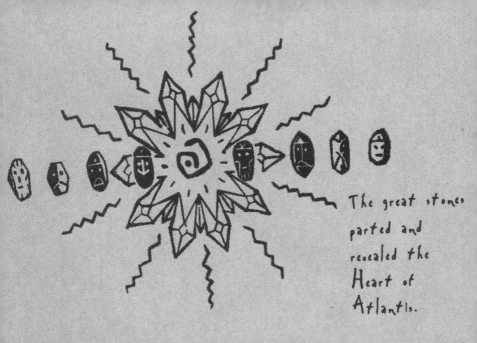

The great stones parted and revealed the Heart of Atlantis.

My excitement at this revelation was instantly crushed when we emerged from the pool to find Rourke and the rest of the crew waiting for us. The crew was heavily armed. It was then I realized what an idiot I had been. This was just another treasure hunt for these mercenaries. And their treasure was the Heart of Atlantis!

Rourke pulled a piece of paper from his boot and held it mockingly before me. I recognized it as a page from the Shepherd's Journal! The missing page! He must have stolen it from the Journal on the return voyage from Iceland with Grandpa.

There were hints of the Heart of Atlantis everywhere in the Shepherd's manuscript, but now that I've seen this page it seems so obvious. I feel so stupid for not piecing this deception together much sooner.

Rourke snapped his fingers. His soldiers organized, and Kida and I were roughly escorted to the palace.

I explained to him that it wasn't a diamond as he thought, or even a battery as I had surmised, but, rather, IT WAS THE LIFE FORCE OF THE ATLANTEAN PEOPLE. I pleaded with him not to continue his mercenary mission.

Entering the king's chamber, Miss Sinclair commanded the troops to search the palace. As his soldiers and crew began to ransack the throne room, Rourke pressed me for more answers. In a careless moment I'll always regret, I stupidly divulged that the Journal revealed "the Heart of Atlantis lies in the eyes of her king."

Rourke assumed that to mean King Kashekim Nedakh, and he and his soldiers surrounded the monarch menacingly. Rourke approached him, demanding to know the whereabouts of the crystal chamber, to which the king calmly replied, "You will destroy yourselves."

Rourke then socked the aging king. This sudden

violence startled the rest of the crew, who stood agape at their commander. Rourke took the place of the fallen king and sat on the throne.

He spotted a beam of light that shone into a reflecting pool. In the pool lay a group of rocks that resembled the symbol on the cover of the Shepherd's Journal. "This is it!" he crowed.

Rourke stepped out into the reflecting pool, and into the beam of light. Miss Sinclair and a still-struggling Kida followed. The water began to vibrate as the commander stepped into the center of the symbol. Suddenly, the symbol began to descend!

Rourke pulled me onto this strange "aquavator," and the four of us slowly descended into the unknown.

The peculiar elevator deposited us in an amazing chamber. Once we stepped off, we saw it—the mother crystal, the Heart of Atlantis, floating high above a placid pool of water. Huge carved stones slowly orbited and protected the great crystal. The crystal's protective stones were carved in the images of mighty faces.

Kida exclaimed at the sight "Ohhh...the kings of our past!" and fell to her knees in prayer.

I knelt down next to her in apology. I felt this predicament was my responsibility! I had led these interlopers to this place.

Rourke stepped to the water's edge and kicked a small stone into the still water. Suddenly the placid blue of the crystal changed to a flaming red, as if it were awakened by Rourke's actions. Bright beams of light emanated from the crystal and searched throughout the chamber.

One of the searching beams of light engulfed Kida, putting her into a trancelike state. The crystal about her neck began to float at the end of its tethering necklace cord. As if in a daze, she walked to the edge of the pool.

Rourke demanded an explanation of what was happening, but all it had said in the Shepherd's Journal was that the crystal was somehow...alive.

How could I explain to a realist like Rourke that this was beyond being a mere engine, like a steam mill or a coal furnace? The Atlanteans were a part of the crystal and it was a part of them. This was truly a power source...a deity.

Kida turned toward us. Her eyes were completely blank, emotionless.

She spoke in an even, deliberate tone. Her voice seemed to echo, but not through the chamber. This echo sounded like it came from within her. "All will be well," she said to me in Atlantean. "Be not afraid."

Then Kida walked out onto the water. As she made her way under the crystal floating high above us, the protective stones that surrounded it began to open, revealing the glowing crystal inside. An intense shaft of light shone down onto her, and Kida began rising into the air! As she reached the crystal's core, the stones began to revolve around her, slowly at first, then more and more rapidly. Then the spinning of the stones began to slow, and finally they came to a stop.

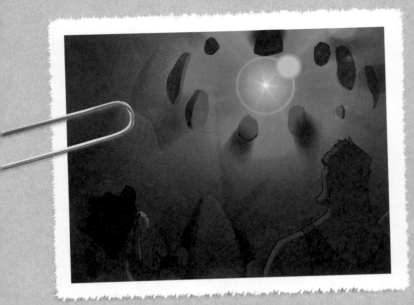

The Heart of Atlantis

Kida slowly descended to the water and I knew, without being able to explain it, that she had become the crystal.

As Kida walked ashore, the huge stones fell and crashed about her. The crystal around her neck now shone with an even brighter light, illuminated from within her.

The crew directed this "crystallized" Kida into a transport pod that began to glow with the crystal's energy. They loaded the pod onto a truck. I watched helplessly as the crew prepared to leave the city. Rourke's soldiers held the assembled Atlanteans—and me—at bay.

I could barely contain my rage, and the flood of other emotions that accompanied an overall sense of utter helplessness. Most of all, I felt betrayed. I had just begun to feel that these people were really my comrades. No, my friends. I couldn't believe they could be a party to this.

I tried to speak to their better selves. I appealed to their better nature. Rourke dismissed me with a snide comment about Darwin and natural selection. I chastised them for going along with Rourke's plans to wipe out an entire civilization for the sake of money. That got their attention.

Miss Sinclair called out to Rourke that all was ready. Rourke turned quickly in my direction and delivered a knockout blow that sent me crashing to the ground.

The photo of me with Grandpa fell from my pocket, and Rourke stepped on it.

Things couldn't get much more symbolic than that.

Rourke ordered the troops to assemble and move out with their ill-gotten cargo. He didn't seem to notice the way in which each crew member was assessing their commander, appraising the situation. He didn't seem to notice the guilt on their faces. I did.

Audrey got in her truck. She stared at the steering wheel. To my great relief she kicked open her truck door and strode over to help me. As Audrey glared at them, the remaining crew— Cookie, Vinny, Mole, even Packard—followed her to my side.

Disgusted, Rourke climbed into his truck and started the engine. Miss Sinclair and the remaining soldiers crossed the bridge, heading toward the escape shaft they had discovered on the other side.

It seemed that as Kida moved farther away from us, I could see the illumination of the city, even the glow of the crystals worn by the individual Atlanteans, begin to dim. I could feel the energy of the city diminish.

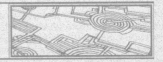

PART SIX

CLIMAX AND AFTERMATH

A long-dormant armada and a dramatic battle
save Atlantis and its citizens from doom.

From where I sit, the risk of hiring privateers
is well worth the specialized skills and
independent spirit they bring to an expedition.
Of course, I'm chagrined from here to next
Tuesday afternoon about what happened with
Rourke, and at a bit of a loss to explain why
someone who spent the better part of a lifetime
as a freebooter would snap at the sight of a
little loot.

After the many adventures that all of these
explorers had shared with Thaddeus Thatch, I
would have given them more credit than to
behave like a pack of drunken sailors, and
treat a place like Atlantis as if it were the
Tenderloin!

In my book, the only thing that separated
this motley crew from a worthless pack of
pirates was the way they responded to a leader.
No, not Rourke, mind you--I mean a true leader.
Milo James Thatch.

Thatch had learned in a few days what
Rourke had not discovered in years of
exploration: Character is more important than
rank, loyalty is more important than wealth,
and what the people who truly know you think is
more important than your status in the eyes of
strangers.

--P.B.W.

Dr. Sweet called me back to the palace. There was alarm in his voice.

I asked about the king's condition, and Sweet's manner was grave. He informed me that the king had suffered much internal bleeding and that there was nothing more he could do. What a nightmare. And I brought it here.

A, I watched over the king, he reached up and grasped my wrist. With a much-weakened voice, he demanded to know where Kida was. I could not answer him.

Yet, he knew. He knew Kida had been chosen, like her mother before her. He explained that in times of danger, the crystal chooses a host, one of royal blood to protect itself and its people. When I asked the king if he meant that the crystal was alive, he revealed that the crystal thrived on the collective emotions of all who came before. In return, it provided power, longevity, and protection. Over time it had developed a consciousness of its own.

His face was pained as he continued. "In my
arrogance, I sought to use it as a weapon of
war...but its power proved too great to control.
It overwhelmed us and led to our destruction."

That's why he hid the crystal beneath
the city—to prevent history from
repeating itself, and to prevent Kida
from suffering the same fate as his
queen. Too late!

The King's last moments.

The king explained that if Kida remained bonded to the crystal, she could be lost to it forever. "But now it falls to you," he instructed me—placing his own crystal in my hands. "Return the crystal. Save the city. Save my daughter."

With that, the king died.

I clutched the king's crystal in my fist. Tears welled in my eyes. "It's been my experience that when you hit bottom," Sweet said quietly, "the only place left to go is up."

"Who told you that?" I snarled back at him.

"Fella by the name of Thaddeus Thatch."

—M.J.T.

When I strode out of the king's chamber, I saw Vinny, Audrey, and the rest of the crew waiting for me.

I told them that I was going after Rourke. Naturally, their reaction was to tell me that my action was crazy, to which I could only come up with one response: I didn't say it was the smart thing, it was the right thing.

I climbed aboard one of the stone fish statues, put the king's crystal into the vehicle keyhole, and the "statue" began to hover.

I could tell that Packard, Audrey, and Vinny were impressed, and as they saw that I knew a little something about what I was doing, they began to rally behind me. The Atlanteans were just as surprised, and

I instructed them how to use their
crystals as Kida had showed me. Everyone
ran for their own stone fish.

The Atlantean Armada ascended skyward!

As we reached the escape shaft, I saw that Rourke had attached the chamber holding the princess to the gondola of a propeller-driven dirigible, and that he and his crew meant to effect their escape by ascending through the caldera of a dormant volcano high above.

We couldn't let them reach the top of that shaft! I could see Kida in the transport pod through a portal. I tried to redirect Rourke's attack so I could reach her.

I hovered next to Rourke and the balloon, and leapt from my fish into the dirigible's netting. As my now unmanned vehicle swept past, I saw it rip a small fissure in the skin of the balloon, causing it to lose altitude.

Rourke commanded Miss Sinclair to lighten the load, and she jettisoned the last of the fuel tanks. But the balloon continued to fall.

Rourke ruthlessly determined to push Miss Sinclair over the side!

I was finally able to reach Rourke in the dirigible gondola and land on him. Obviously, I have never been much of a pugilist, but I tried to strike out at Rourke, who caught my fist and pushed it back into my face. I think he kicked me then, for I found myself flying into (and through) the balloon's side railing. As I dangled precariously from the railing, I reached for the chain that held Kida's imprisoning pod.

The last vestiges of Rourke's military composure gave way to a roaring fury. To escape his wrath, I swung like a monkey from chain to chain, as Rourke followed me.

Suddenly, the dirigible was on fire! Rourke broke a glass cabinet that contained a fire axe, which I considered a curious action to take until I realized he was flailing with the axe at me!

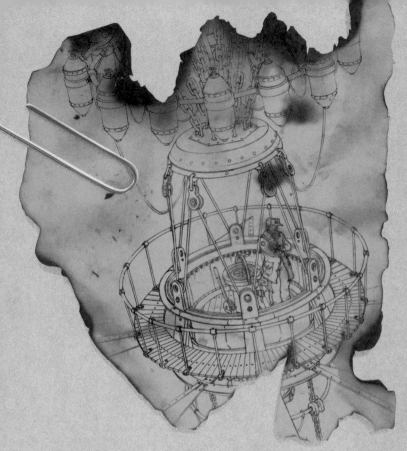

Examining the wreckage I found this page
from the balloon "owners's" manual

    In one of his wild swings, Rourke smashed the
window of Kida's transport pod. I snatched up a
shard of broken glass, which was still glowing with
crystal energy. At that moment, Rourke finally
caught me, and as he took me by the throat, I
slashed at his arm with the energized glass.

Rourke's arm, and then his entire body, began to crystallize! However, instead of the pure and soothing blue that engulfed Kida, Rourke turned red and black, and hardened like a burnt ember!

Suddenly Rourke seemed to reanimate and reached for me. Deftly, I maneuvered so that I led what was left of Rourke to move backward into the dirigible's swinging steering blades, smashing him into smithereens.

The chain holding the transport pod broke and fell to the ground. I leapt from the balloon and managed to land on the pod, out of the way as the balloon descended and exploded in a fiery inferno.

From my vantage point, the force of the explosion created fissures in the ground, fractures that spread like spider legs from the point of impact. The force of the explosion ended this volcanic flue's dormancy, and molten lava began to erupt from these fissures.

Now the most important rescue was not our own, but that of Kida. We had to return her to her city or all of Atlantis would die!

I must say I don't recall what my companions now describe as my heroic evasion of erupting lava as I reattached the chain around the transport pod and held on. I was of a single purpose then, and my own safety didn't come into my mind. I held on to the pod for dear life as we again ascended on our vehicles. We raced back through the caves to reach the city.

Hurtling out of the last cave just ahead of the lava, we sailed to the central plaza, managing to land and guide the transport pod down safely. Borrowing an Atlantean spear, I pried a small part of the pod open. The walls of the pod flew off, revealing the captive princess. Kida hovered in the plaza.

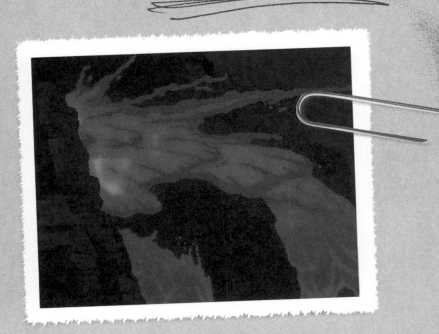

Suddenly the Heart of Atlantis's protective stones broke through the plaza center's surface. They must have been brought back to life by the return of Kida's energy.

I tried to run to her, but was stopped by a stone rising from the ground. The stones surrounded the princess, and all began to ascend above the city.

The stones once again orbited Kida. As they spun she became brighter and brighter, electric beams emanated from her body.

As in a day of endless wonders, there was still another spectacular miracle to be witnessed. These beams activated giant fallen stone statues throughout the city. These statues began to rise out of the water, energized by the beams. Once standing, they formed a towering circle around the city.

Stone Giant

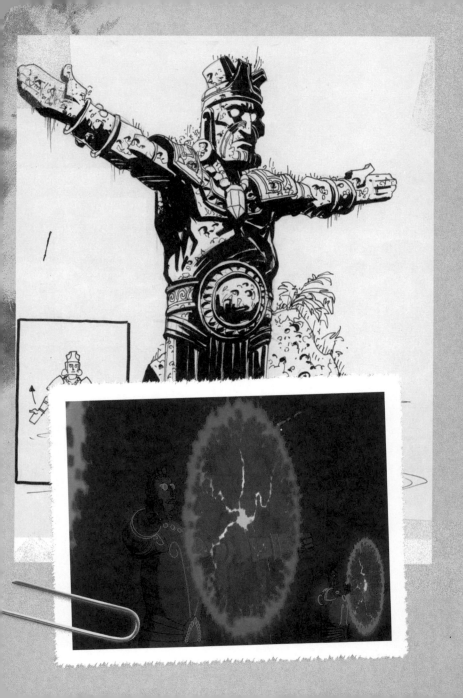

We stood in awe as the Giants' protective shield withstood the cataclysm.

Just as lava broke through the cave walls, these giant stone guardians clapped their hands, creating an engulfing dome of energy that covered the city. Though a huge lava wave engulfed Atlantis, this protective shield of energy held firm. The city was safe.

Kida returns.

Kida slowly descended and made a perfect landing into my waiting arms. The first word she spoke was my name. We embraced, overcome with emotion. The lava dome fell away leaving a new, beautiful Atlantis—the hidden Atlantis of the past, more dazzling than ever before, had risen. Kida grasped my hand in hers, and I knew that I had found a new home.

—M.J.T.

The rest of my crew is leaving Atlantis today. I have decided to stay on. Dr. Sweet asked me if I was sure I wanted to remain here. He believed a hero's welcome awaits "the man who discovered Atlantis."

I don't think the world needs another hero. Besides, I told the doctor mischievously, there was a need down here for an "expert in gibberish."

We're gathered at the central plaza center to say farewell. The Atlanteans are loading a stone fish with all sorts of treasures. They will escort the visitors as far as the surface.

Kida thanked the crew. "Atlantis will honor your names forever."

I wish I could do as much for them as they have done for a shy, bookish, insecure academic, who has realized his scholastic dreams and personal wishes tenfold.

I will miss them all. We have been through a series of miraculous adventures, to be sure, but the memories of those adventures are vivid and palpable, and I will carry them with me through the rest of my life.

More important, I am saddened because I can only carry a memory of their eccentric personalities and convivial good humor. I will miss the feeling of their affection and their respect for me.

For me this was the most important
treasure I discovered upon this expedition.

One final thought...

There are men who read of history in
dusty books and speak of antiquity in
dusty halls, never realizing that history
isn't dusty at all. History is a life lived
so fully that what is left behind causes
others to contemplate, to examine, and
to enrich their own lives because of it.

Milo James Thatch

Whitmore Industries

AFTERWORD

After the return of the expedition, I gathered its few remaining members in my study for a debriefing. They had brought back an impressive array of photographs and artifacts. Each of them wore a sparkling Atlantean crystal as jewelry, except Cookie--he was, however, sporting a glittering new crystal tooth.

As I perused the photos of their adventure, I admonished this little crew: "Let's go over it again, just so we've got it straight. You didn't find anything."

A discovery of such magnitude, a power source of such enormity, and the damage the secrets of Atlantis could do to the world (let alone the danger it might cause those who were the custodians of those secrets)... Well, the whole darn thing was just too dangerous to reveal to the world... especially the way the world was looking in those darkening days toward the end of 1914.

Fortunately, the assembled group agreed with me, and I had no reason to doubt their integrity. I ran through a few questions that I knew might arise.

What happened to Helga Sinclair? "Missing."

Rourke? "Missing, too."

What about Milo Thatch? "He went down with the sub."

I unwrapped a package addressed to me that this crew had brought back. It contained a dazzling crystal necklace and a journal along with this note from young Thatch.

I wear that crystal around my neck to this very day, with immeasurable honor and unending pride.

I'm going to miss that boy. At least he's in a better place now.

You know, I have never been happier to lose a bet in my entire life.

--P.B.W.